The School Mouse

Dick King-Smith
Illustrated by Cynthia Fisher

Hyperion Books for Children
New York

Text © 1995 by Dick King-Smith.
Illustrations © 1995 by Cynthia Fisher.

Printed in the United States of America.

First Edition
3 5 7 9 10 8 6 4 2

The artwork for each picture is prepared using pen and ink,
and watercolor wash on Arches.
This book is set in 16-point Bembo.
Designed by Mara Van Fleet.

Library of Congress Cataloging-in-Publication Data
King-Smith, Dick.
The school mouse / Dick King-Smith ; illustrated by
Cynthia Fisher. — 1st ed.
p.   cm.
Summary: Flora, the world's most educated mouse,
saves her family during a crisis.
ISBN 0-7868-0036-4 (trade)—ISBN 0-7868-2029-2 (lib. bdg.)
[1. Mice—Fiction. 2. Reading—Fiction. 3. Schools—Fiction.
4. Family life—Fiction.] I. Fisher, Cynthia, ill. II. Title.
PZ7.K616Sc   1995
[Fic]—dc20   94-48443

Contents

 CHAPTER ONE

In Which Flora Makes a Start

FLORA WAS A SCHOOL MOUSE.

Everyone knows that there are house mice and field mice and harvest mice, and everyone knows that mice who live inside churches are called church mice. So it's easy to guess where Flora lived.

The school was a very old one, nearly a hundred and fifty years old in fact, and it stood in the middle of some fields.

Forty-two children went to the school (kindergartners, first graders, second graders), and about the same number of mice (fathers, mothers, and children) lived permanently in its crumbly old walls and ceilings and dark cupboards, and under its worn wooden floorboards.

But of all these school mice, only one grew up to become interested in learning the same lessons as the children.

That was Flora.

It was as though Flora was destined to be a very special school mouse, for she was born on the first day of the first half of the new school year, in a hole in the wall of the kindergarten classroom.

Immediately behind the teacher's desk there was a cupboard set into the old white-washed stone wall, and just above the doors of this cupboard there was a small space between two of the stones. High up inside the cupboard a hole had been gnawed, so that a school mouse could run up inside and make its way into the space between the stones. From here, if it peeped out, it would have a fine view of the classroom, including a close-up of the top of the teacher's head, a couple of feet below, as she sat at her desk.

On this particular morning a particular school mouse did not peep out at the kindergarten classroom, for it was much too busy giving birth to ten babies, one of which was the infant Flora.

All that day the mother mouse lay in the hole in the wall and suckled her new pink naked babies until school was ended and the children had gone home and the cleaning ladies had tidied up and the care-taker had locked up and the old school was empty of all life save for the jackdaws nesting in the chimneys and the school mice.

Then, at last easing herself off her sleeping babies, the mother scuttled down into the cupboard and out between its rickety old doors that never quite shut. One jump landed her on top of the teacher's desk and another onto her chair, down the leg of which she clambered.

In the middle of the classroom floor, she could see, was another mouse, pottering about, whiskers twitching. He was searching for any little bits of anything eatable that the children might have dropped and the cleaning ladies missed.

What a husband, thought the mother mouse, whose name was Hyacinth. Here am I, brought to bed of ten children, and he's not even been to visit me. And sharply she called out, "Robin!"

Hyacinth's husband was an untidy fellow whose coat always looked badly in need of grooming. He had lost part of one ear in a fight and the end of his tail in a trap, and the other school mice called him Ragged

Robin. Now, at Hyacinth's summons, he came hurrying toward her.

"Hyce!" he cried (for it was his habit always to address his wife thus—to rhyme with "mice"). "Hyce, my love! I haven't seen you all day!"

"No," said Hyacinth shortly.

"And you seem to have grown thinner, more slender, that is," said Robin.

"Yes," said Hyacinth.

"Have you been on a diet?"

"No," said Hyacinth. "I have simply lost weight."

"How?" said Robin.

"You had better come and see."

Up the leg of the teacher's chair they went and onto the desktop and up inside the cupboard to the hole in the wall.

"There!" said Hyacinth, and she could not keep a note of pride from her voice. "All yours!"

"All mine?" said Ragged Robin, and he could not keep a note of anxiety from his voice. Did she expect him to look after this swarm of ugly little pink hairless monsters? He had never had children before. What did fathers do?

"What do I do, Hyce?" he asked nervously.

"Do?" said Hyacinth. "You don't do anything. It is I who have to suckle them and keep them warm and keep them clean and bring them up to be good mousekins. All you need to do is admire our ten children. Are they not beautiful?"

"Without doubt," said Robin doubtfully. "Ten, did you say?" he asked.

"Yes, as alike as peas in a pod."

But here, though she was not to know it for quite a while, Hyacinth was wrong.

Alike in looks and size the babies might be, and no one, watching them as their hair grew and their eyes opened and they began to crawl about the nest, could possibly have told one from another. Yet among them, as the weeks went by and they grew into active nimble mousekins, was one, a female, who was to develop into the world's most educated school mouse.

That one, of course, was Flora.

Whether in fact Flora was more intelligent than her nine brothers and sisters we shall never know. What is certain is that she was more inquisitive. From an early age Flora liked to poke her nose into everything. Everything interested her, and "why" was her favorite word. Why did they live in a school? Why was the school sometimes full of people, mostly small, and why sometimes empty? Why did all these small people, and some big ones, come to the school? Why did the little ones look at lots of pieces of paper all joined together, with pictures on them and strange black marks and squiggles on the white paper? Why did they hold what looked like thin pieces of wood in their fat little hands and make other black marks on other sheets of paper?

All these things Flora observed, for she alone looked outward from the hole in the wall above the teacher's desk in the kindergarten classroom. Always during the school day Hyacinth and the other nine kept well back inside, out of sight, but Flora crouched at the dark mouth of the hole, watching everything that went on with the greatest curiosity.

Whether she inherited this thirst for knowledge from her matter-of-fact mother or her somewhat scatterbrained father we shall, again, never know, but it did not take her long to discover that neither of them knew the answers to all her many "why's." It was up to her to find out. She began the very next morning.

One thing that Flora already knew was that at some time in each day each child came to stand beside the teacher's desk, directly below her. The child would bring with it one of those joined-together wads of paper and put it down on the desk and open it. Then the teacher would point at the black marks on the paper, one after another, from left to right, and the child would make different noises.

Day after day Flora peered down intently,

longing to make sense of whatever was going on. But her eyes, though clearly seeing the shape of the printed words on the pages of the reading books, could not interpret them. And her ears, though clearly hearing the child as it read, could not understand the sounds it made.

Then, at last, one morning came the great breakthrough that was to make all the difference to Flora's future.

She was watching attentively as usual while a little girl stood beside the teacher with her reading book. She was a very little girl, just beginning to learn to read, and the book was a very simple one. On each page was a large colored picture and below the picture a single word.

The first picture, for example, was of a round red fruit, and below it was written

Apple

Flora had never seen an apple, so the sound the child made meant nothing to her, nor had she yet in her short life set eyes on a loaf of

Bread

or (mercifully) on a

C a t

or on any of the other objects shown as the pages turned. Until the child reached *M*.

There was a picture that Flora immediately recognized, and below it were five little black marks on the paper, five marks like these:

M o u s e

"Well?" said the teacher.

"Mouse," said the child, and in Flora's tiny brain something clicked.

Once again she stared hungrily at those five little black marks.

"Mouse," she said to herself.

Flora had begun to read.

CHAPTER TWO

In Which Flora Reads a Story

THE FIVE LETTERS, EACH SO different from its fellows, that made up that first word were the key to Flora's progress.

As she crouched in the hole in the wall, eagerly watching the children reading from their various books, she began to recognize those strangely shaped black marks. This was especially so when one of them was the first letter of a word that meant something to her.

The shape *M,* for example, stood not only for "mouse" but for "mother." *O* was for "owl," and though Flora had never seen one, Hyacinth had told them all what made that melancholy nighttime cry outside the old school. And *U* began a number of common words like "us" and "up" and "under," while *S* was for lots of things mice did, like "squeak" and "scurry" and "sniff," and *E* for another, most important one, "eat."

One word led to another, and since Flora not only looked but also listened as each of the children read to the teacher every day, she began to match the shape of the word on the page to the sound that came out of the child's mouth.

Never was there such an attentive, hard-working school mouse as Flora. As winter vacation approached, something else happened that was to further Flora's education.

One weekend, a time when the school mice had the place to themselves, Hyacinth called a family conference in the cupboard in the kindergarten classroom.

Ragged Robin had taken little notice of his ten children, being too busy, like all his fellows, searching for food. But now, summoned by his wife, he gave the mousekins his full attention.

"I say, Hyce!" he cried. "I must congratulate you, my love. You have reared ten splendid children. How strong and healthy they look."

"They are," said Hyacinth. "Say hello to Daddy, children."

"Hello, Daddy!" chorused the mouse-kins—all except Flora, who said, "Hello, *Father,*" a word that she had recently learned.

"And now," said Hyacinth, "say good-bye."

"To Daddy?" asked one of the children.

"To both of us," said Hyacinth. "It is time you all went to seek your fortunes out in the great wide school."

"Yippee!" cried nine of the mousekins, and away they went, out of the cupboard, onto the desk, onto the floor, and out through one or the other of the doors of the kindergarten classroom, rejoicing that they were kindergartners no longer.

Only Flora remained. She did not at all wish her education to be interrupted.

"Mother," she said. "Please can I stay here? I like it here. I wouldn't be in your way."

"You won't," said Hyacinth, "because I'm not staying. That hole in the wall is drafty. I'm off to find somewhere cozier for the next brood."

"Next brood, Hyce?" said Robin. "Next brood of what?"

"Babies, you booby," said Hyacinth crossly. "Hadn't you noticed?"

Ragged Robin looked at his wife. "You seem to have put on weight—grown plumper, that is," he said. "I had not realized."

"Hadn't you," said Hyacinth.

"Another lot of babies," said Robin thoughtfully. "And so soon. I don't know how you do it, Hyce."

Hyacinth looked at her scruffy husband with an expression that was a mixture of scorn and resignation.

"Run along, Robin, do," she said, "and see if you can find somewhere really comfortable for me. Preferably not in one of the other classrooms—children are so noisy."

"Right ho, Hyce," said Ragged Robin. "I'll try the staff room first. Meet me there." And off he went.

"Now, young lady," said Hyacinth, "just what is this all about? You saw how anxious your brothers and sisters were to be gone. Why do you want to stay here?"

"Please, mother," said Flora, "it's a good place for my lessons."

"Lessons?"

"Yes, Mother. I'm learning to read."

"To read?" said Hyacinth. "What on earth does that mean?"

"To make sense of the words in books, Mother. It's what the schoolchildren are taught to do. They are learning to read, and so am I. It's very interesting. At first I could only read the odd word here and there, but before long I hope to be able to read a whole story."

"Flora!" said Hyacinth sternly. "I haven't the foggiest idea what you're talking about except that it's rubbish. Who ever heard of mice doing the same things that people do. Next thing, you'll be walking about on your hind legs. You listen to me, my girl— just forget all this nonsense. You've got too high an opinion of yourself; that's your trouble. Giving yourself airs and making out you're cleverer than the rest of us. You're just an ordinary school mouse, and don't you forget it." And with this Hyacinth went out through the cupboard doors and dropped, carefully, because of the burden she was carrying, down to the desk and onto the floor and away.

Flora climbed up to the hole in the wall and looked out at the kindergarten classroom. Empty as it was of humans and mice, there was no one to hear her say, "I am not an ordinary school mouse. I'm sure I'm not. I'm sure I can learn all sorts of things that no mouse has ever learned before, if only I study hard enough, and then I shall be an extraordinary school mouse."

The next day dawned. Flora never forgot that first Monday morning all on her own in the kindergarten classroom. Not that the other mousekins had interrupted her studies—they and their mother had mostly slept during school hours—but it was lovely to feel she had the place to herself now, ready for another happy week's work.

As if to celebrate her independence, she did something she had never before dared to do.

At midday the bell rang for lunch, and the children lined up and then left the classroom, followed by the teacher. On her desk, by chance, a reading book had been left wide open, and Flora, seeing this, slipped down and stood before it, her little forepaws upon the edge of the page.

How big and bright the pictures were, now that she was so close. How bold and black the words!

By great good luck the book, called *Billy's Pet,* was open at page one, and when Flora had read that and page two opposite, she very much wanted to know what happened next. But of course there was no one to turn over the pages.

Billy, the boy in the story, wanted a pet of his own. "But is Billy old enough," his father asked his mother, "to look after a pet properly?"

Is he? thought Flora. Will they let him have one? And if they do, what will it be? A rabbit? A gerbil? A guinea pig? What color will it be? What will it be called?

I must know, thought Flora, and carefully she poked her nose under page two and flipped it over. Once she had the knack of page turning, keeping each flat with a foot as she read, it was easy. By the time the children came in from the playground at the end of the lunch hour, Flora was safely back in the hole in the wall. On the desk *Billy's Pet* lay open, at the last two pages now.

Flora looked down contentedly. "I must confess," she said to herself, "I do like a happy ending."

CHAPTER THREE

In Which Sweet William Makes a Mistake

A HAPPY ENDING WAS NOT IN store for Flora's brothers and sisters. Unlike her, they were excitable and rather thoughtless mousekins, and for them, life was to be short and death brutal.

Several, scavenging for food, ventured outside the walls of the school that week, never to come in again. A hungry fox, sniffing around the garbage cans, snapped up one of them and the owls put paid to two more, while a fourth mousekin fell into the goldfish pond and drowned.

As for the survivors, they ran about the school as though they owned the place, squeaking with glee at their newfound freedom.

Foolish behavior like this was bound, sooner or later, to threaten the safety of all the other school mice, and in fact it was one of Flora's remaining brothers, a scapegrace by the name of Sweet William, who did the deed that was to lead to unhappy endings for so many.

If there's one thing that mice love, it's chocolate, and Sweet William had come upon a dusty red candy that some child had dropped under a desk in the second grade.

This was the class that the headmistress taught, and after his meal Sweet William climbed up onto her desk and began to clean his whiskers. Whether it was on account of the rich meal he had eaten or whether he did it out of bravado we shall never know, but the fact remains that Sweet William positioned himself on top of the big blue class register that lay on the desk, and in the middle of it he did several rather sticky droppings.

At first, when the second graders came into their classroom next morning, no one noticed, but then a sharp-eyed boy spotted the little browny-yellow objects.

"Hey, look everybody!" he called.

"What is it?" said everybody.

The discoverer pointed proudly. "Mouse poo," he said, "all over the register."

"Ugh!" cried several, and then there was a chorus of voices.

"She'll go mad when she sees them!"

"Put them in the wastepaper basket, then."

"No, you're not allowed to touch the register."

"Leave them, leave them, see what she says!"

"Shh! Look out! She's coming!"

Everybody rushed to their places as the headmistress came in and closed the classroom door. Every eye was on her. No one moved a muscle. As she sat down at the desk and put out a hand to open the register you could have heard a pin drop. Then she saw what Sweet William had dropped. As she looked, with an expression of disgust on her face, the tension in the classroom became electric, and when someone giggled, it set them all off.

"Be quiet!" snapped the headmistress, and instinctively she looked at the naughtiest boy in the class.

"Tommy," she said, "come here." And when he came she pointed at the blue cardboard cover of the register and said, "What do you know about this?"

"Please, miss," said Tommy. "It's mouse poo."

"Did you put it there?"

"No, miss. I never. Honest."

"Then who did?" said the headmistress. She looked round the class again and picked on the most sensible of the girls.

"Heather," she said, "who did this?"

And Heather sensibly answered, "A mouse, miss," and the giggles broke out again.

At morning break the news flashed around the playground, and soon everyone had heard—everyone, that is, except the school mice. They were not to know that, thanks to Sweet William, the headmistress was at that moment on the phone to city hall, demanding to speak to the pest control officer.

Because the old school was so small, the headmistress's office was just a corner of the staff room, in which at that moment there were no teachers but only, though the headmistress did not know it, eleven mice.

Ragged Robin had found Hyacinth an excellent, snug nesting place under the staff-room floorboards. The entry to it was via a hole in the baseboard, and in it lay Robin, Hyacinth, and nine new babies, safe and comfortable and practically under the headmistress's feet.

The two adult school mice listened dozily but, of course, without understanding to the human voice above.

"I need you to send someone out here immediately," the headmistress was saying. "No, I have no idea how many mice. All I know is that there were mouse droppings on my desk this morning, and winter vacation is almost upon us, and if nothing is done before then we shall have a plague of the creatures come spring. What's that? You'll send a what? A rodent operative? When? Not until vacation begins? Why not? I see. All right. Thank you. Good-bye."

And good-bye it would have been for every school mouse in the place, had it not been for Flora and her newfound skills.

On the first day of winter vacation a man arrived at the school and was admitted by the caretaker.

"You the rat catcher, then?" he said.

"Rodent operative," said the rodent operative a trifle huffily.

"Fuss about nothing," said the caretaker.

"You always get a few mice in a building as old as this, right out in the fields like it is."

"I'll soon get rid of them," said the rodent operative.

"Traps, is it?" said the caretaker.

"No, no. Something tasty for the little devils to eat. That's why I didn't come sooner after it was reported. Don't want kids picking the stuff up and putting it in their mouths. You got a cat or a dog?"

"No."

"Good. Right. I'll get on with it if you'll show me around."

In every room of the old school the rodent operative laid his baits. He opened a number of packets and out of each sprinkled a quantity of little blue pellets onto a piece of cardboard. When a packet was empty, he put the plastic envelope in his pocket. By chance he came to the kindergarten classroom last, and because he was chatting to the caretaker for a moment before taking his leave, he forgot about the final empty packet and left it lying on the teacher's desk. It lay there under the gaze of two sharp eyes from the hole in the wall above.

When the men were gone and the

school silent again, Flora ran down onto the desk and looked curiously, first at the piece of cardboard on which was a cluster of strange little blue pellets, and then at the plastic packet. There were words printed on it. Flora read them.

First, in big letters, it said

MUSMORS

What does that mean? thought Flora, and she read on.

WARNING:
KEEP MUSMORS AWAY FROM
CHILDREN AND FROM DOGS,
CATS, AND OTHER DOMESTIC
PETS. IF TAKEN IN ERROR,
CONSULT YOUR DOCTOR. NO
OTHER POISON KILLS THESE
PESTS AS QUICKLY.

MUSMORS IS DEATH TO ALL
MICE!

CHAPTER FOUR

In Which Flora Saves the Day

"THANK GOODNESS I HAVE learned to read," said Flora, "or else I might well have sampled these attractive-looking blue pellets."

But then the thought occurred to her that perhaps there were other poison baits in other parts of the school that other mice might come upon. Even now her mother and father might have found a heap of Musmors. And neither of them could read!

"There is no time to be lost," said Flora, and she scuttled out of the kindergarten classroom as fast as she could go.

Never before had Flora ventured out into other places in the school, and even had she known her way about, she had no idea where her mother and father might be.

Then suddenly she remembered her father's words. "I'll try the staff room first," he had said. That, then, was the most likely place to find them. But wherever was the staff room?

Running along a passageway, Flora came to an open door and, peeping in, could see by the number of tables and chairs and the blackboard and a teacher's desk like the one below the hole in the wall, that it was another classroom.

It was, though Flora could not know this, the first-grade classroom, and on one of the tables, she could see, was a mouse. It was sitting up on its haunches, and in its paws it held something blue!

"Stop! Stop!" squeaked Flora, and running up the leg of the table, she came face-to-face with her brother Sweet William.

"Hello, Flora," he said, picking up another pellet. "Long time no see."

"Oh, stop!" cried Flora again. "How many of those things have you eaten?"

"Quite a lot," said Sweet William, "but don't worry, there are still plenty left. Help yourself."

"No, no!" said Flora.

Uh-oh, she thought: Musmors is death to all mice. Poor Sweet William. There is nothing I can do for him now. But what of my parents? I may yet be in time.

"Mother and Father," she said. "Where are they?"

"Haven't a clue," said Sweet William, munching on yet another pellet. "Matter of fact, I haven't set eyes on any of the family for ages. Why?"

"I must find them," said Flora.

She looked sadly at her brother. "Good-bye," she said softly, but Sweet William was too busy gorging himself to answer.

On the opposite side of the corridor was another classroom, that of the second grade, and there Flora found a spine-chilling scene. There were two separate heaps of the blue pellets, each on its piece of cardboard, and each surrounded by a group of school mice, all busy stuffing themselves with Musmors.

Hastily Flora ran round them, looking, but her mother and father were not among them. She could see, though, four more of her brothers and sisters, and to them, though she knew it was already too late, she cried, "Don't eat that stuff!"

"Push off!" growled several older, strange school mice, and one of them made a dash at her, threatening to bite.

Frantically Flora continued her search,

and everywhere the scene was the same. In the hall, in the library area, in the kitchens, in every corridor and passage, there were little heaps of the poison bait, each with one or more school mice in attendance.

In one passage she found two doors. Both were shut, but each carried a notice that she could read. Boys, one said and the other, Girls.

Is Father in one and Mother in the other? she thought. Oh, where could they be? Would she be in time? But no—they were nowhere, it seemed.

And then at long last she came upon a door, an open door, on which was written Staff Room. Flora dashed in. In one corner of the room was a big desk. On it was the usual cardboard with its heap of blue pellets. And on it, too, was a mouse, an untidy-looking mouse with a battered ear and a tipless tail, who even at that moment was approaching the bait.

"Father!" squealed Flora in an agony of mind. "Wait!" And she rushed across the staff-room floor and up onto the desk and interposed herself between Ragged Robin and certain death.

"Who are you?" said Robin.

"I'm your daughter. Flora. You know, the one that stayed behind in the hole in the wall. Oh, thank goodness I got here in time!"

"Time for what?" said Robin.

"To save your lives," said Flora, for she could see that this pile of blue pellets was as yet untouched.

What is she talking about? thought Robin, scratching his good ear with a hind foot, and as usual when things had got too much for him, he handed the matter over to his wife.

"Hyce!" he cried, and from under the floorboards a voice replied, "What is it?"

"Come up here," called Robin. "It's our Flora. She says she's come to save our lives."

In a moment or so Hyacinth appeared at the mouth of the hole in the baseboard and made her way up onto the desktop.

"What's the matter?" she said grumpily. "I've got nine children to feed, you know, and what are you doing here, young lady, and what's all this about saving our lives, and what's that heap of blue pellets?"

"They're poison, Mother," said Flora.

"Poison?"

"Special stuff for killing mice. My brothers and sisters have eaten it and they are going to die, and if you and Father eat it, you will both die, and then all your nine new mousekins will die, and last of all," cried Flora dramatically, "I shall die! Of a broken heart!"

"Pull yourself together, child," said Hyacinth. "How do you know this stuff kills mice?"

"I read it," said Flora. "On the packet. I told you, I've learned to read, just like people do. You wouldn't believe me before, but please believe me now, Mother! I don't want to be an orphan!"

Hyacinth sniffed at the blue pellets. "They look attractive," she said. "Smell nice, too."

"That's just it," said Flora. "That's what all the other school mice are saying, and soon they'll all be dead! You just wait and see."

"Load of nonsense," said Ragged Robin. "They look good, those things. The child doesn't know what she's talking about. Let's try some, Hyce."

"No!" said Hyacinth sharply. "We'll do what Flora says. We'll wait and see. We'll wait a day or so, and then we'll see if one single mouse in the school has died from eating this stuff. And if by any chance it has, then I shall begin to believe in this 'reading' that Flora's always on about. How long is it supposed to take this stuff to work?"

"I don't know," Flora replied. "It just said 'quickly.'"

"Load of nonsense," said Robin again.

"We'll see," said Hyacinth. "In the meantime, don't you touch it, understand?"

"Yes, Hyce," said Robin.

"And as for you, young lady," said Hyacinth, "you look to me as if you could do with a good day's sleep. Off you go now, and we'll have a meeting here in the staff room tomorrow."

On her way back to the hole in the wall Flora passed the open door of the second-grade classroom and saw that Sweet William was no longer on the table that had held the Musmors. Nor were there any pellets left on it. He had eaten the lot.

But somewhere in the classroom someone was groaning horribly.

Flora fled.

CHAPTER FIVE

In Which Flora Moves Up a Grade

THE MEETING IN THE STAFF room the next day was a grim one.

Flora had run all the way from the kindergarten classroom, not daring to look into either of the others as she passed. But she couldn't help noticing, as she crossed the hall, that the pieces of cardboard there were bare of bait. It had all been eaten.

In the staff room her worst fears were confirmed by her father. Hyacinth had sent him out on a tour of the entire school, and he had shortly arrived back.

"We are alone!" Flora heard him saying in funereal tones.

"No, we're not," said Hyacinth briskly. "Here's Flora coming."

"That is not what I meant," said Ragged Robin. "We—that is, you and me and

Flora and the nine mousekins—are alone in the school."

"What?" said Hyacinth. "Has everyone else left?"

"Everyone else," said Robin, "is dead."

There was a silence. Robin had said his piece, Flora had nothing to add, and Hyacinth was thinking.

At last she spoke. "Flora, my girl," Hyacinth said, "I owe you an apology. You have indeed saved our lives."

"It's just lucky that I can read, Mother," Flora said.

"Read something for us now," said Hyacinth.

Flora looked around the staff room. On one wall was a board with a great many notices pinned on it. But it was too far away for her to read the print. However, on the wall immediately behind her was a sign with two large words on it, in red. Flora pointed her muzzle at it.

"See that?" she said.

"Yes," they answered.

"Well, that says No Smoking."

"What does that mean?" they asked.

"I don't know," said Flora. "But I daresay

I shall find out one day. There are an awful lot of things I don't know."

"Well, I'll tell you something that *I* know, beyond the shadow of a doubt," said Hyacinth, "and that is that we are leaving school."

"Leaving?" said Ragged Robin. "Why?"

"Because," said Hyacinth, "the people here obviously think that the only good school mouse is a dead school mouse, and they won't rest till they've killed us, too. In another few days the mousekins will be old enough to travel, and then we're off. All of us. Understood?"

"Yes," said Robin.

"No," said Flora.

"What was that?" said Hyacinth.

"No, Mother," said Flora. "I'm sorry, but I'm not coming. I've only had half a year of school, and I've got a great deal still to learn."

"I'll say you have," said Hyacinth sharply. "I told you once before, my girl, you think too highly of yourself. You just do as I tell you."

"No, Mother," said Flora.

Hyacinth turned on Robin. "Well?" she

said. "Have you no control over the child?"

Robin looked thoughtful. "No, Hyce," he said.

"For the last time, Flora," said Hyacinth, "are you coming with us or not?"

"No," said Flora.

"Right!" snapped Hyacinth. "On your own head be it! I now declare this meeting closed." And she disappeared into the hole in the baseboard.

Before winter vacation ended, two things happened.

First, the rodent operative paid a return visit to the school.

And second, the staff room was once more free of mice. Hyacinth, Ragged Robin, and their nine new mousekins had emigrated.

"I've been picking up dead mice everywhere," said the caretaker when he let the rodent operative in. "That stuff of yours did the trick all right. They lapped it up, they did. It's all gone, barring two baits: one in the staff room and one in here, in the kindergarten classroom. They weren't touched—don't know why."

"Funny," said the rodent operative. He tipped the uneaten Musmors into an envelope. Then he caught sight of the hole in the wall above the teacher's desk. He put his nose to it and sniffed.

"One in there?" said the caretaker.

The rodent operative nodded. He opened the cupboard doors and, looking in, saw the other entrance to Flora's hiding place.

"Watch out inside here," he said, and he took from his pocket a long thin gadget like a buttonhook and poked it hard into the hole in the wall. But when he pulled it back out again, all it brought with it was a tangle of old nesting material. Flora had moved up a grade.

Not until the caretaker had picked up the corpses, including that of poor Sweet William, had Flora been able to force herself to enter the first-grade classroom. But she was determined to continue with her education, and she reasoned that it was time for her to move up in the school. After all, she thought, I am older now.

It was too much to hope that there

would be another conveniently placed hole in the wall, and indeed there wasn't. But Flora was in luck nevertheless. Behind the teacher's desk was a long bookshelf. Like all mice, Flora could run up a sheer wall if it was roughcast and not too high, and she got up onto this shelf without much trouble.

The books on it were loosely arranged, and squeezing between two of them, Flora found that the shelf was so deep that there was plenty of room behind—room and to spare for a school mouse keen to continue with her studies. She would be able to run up and down behind the line of books and peep out wherever there was a space.

I'll be better off than when I was in kindergarten, she thought. I'll be able to look down on a number of the children's tables as well as the teacher's desk. And there's a nice view of the blackboard.

Flora waited anxiously for school to begin again. On the day before it began there was a staff meeting.

"One final thing," said the headmistress to the kindergarten teacher and the first-grade teacher and the part-timer who came in two days a week to take the second graders, "that I know you'll be glad to hear. We are all animal lovers, I'm sure, but I'm happy to tell you that city hall sent a man during vacation who has exterminated all the mice. There is not a mouse alive anywhere in this school, not one."

But there was.

CHAPTER SIX

In Which Hyacinth Leads the Way

HYACINTH HAD NOT MADE the decision to leave school lightly. She was aware that to journey with her family to some new, as yet unknown, home would be a hazardous business.

But already, it seemed, she had lost nine children, her entire first litter of mousekins save for that stubborn girl Flora, and she did not want to lose another nine. For her the school was now a place of death, and it was her duty to take them abroad, whatever the risks.

"And it is your duty to accompany us," she said to her husband.

"But Hyce . . . ," began Ragged Robin.

"No buts," said Hyacinth.

So it was that some nights after the great massacre, Hyacinth led the way out of the staff room, out of the school, across the playground, and into the fields.

Following her in single file came the nine mousekins, while a nervous Robin brought up the rear, casting fearful glances all around him as they threaded their way through the darkness.

For some reason it had tickled Hyacinth's fancy to give to her second litter names beginning with the same letter, and as soon as they were clear of the school grounds she took a roll call.

"Lily?" she called.

"Here, Mom."

"Lilac? Lotus? Lupin?"

"Here, Mom." "Here, Mom." "Here, Mom."

"Lobelia? Laburnum? Larkspur? Lavender?" and there was a chorus of "Here, Mom's."

"Now, who have I left out?"

"Me, Mom," piped a little voice.

"Who are you?"

"Love-in-a-Mist, Mom."

"And me, Hyce," said a rather hurt voice.

"Yes, yes, and you, Robin," said Hyacinth. "Now, then, keep close together, nose to tail, and not a squeak out of any of you." Or the owls will get you, she thought. I only hope we can find shelter before long. I can't think how field mice manage, living out here.

Walking across even a large field is nothing to a human being, but the mousekins soon wearied of battling their way through the long grass. Despite whispers of "Shhh, darlings," from Hyacinth and "Keep it quiet, kids," from their father, there was soon a chorus of unhappy cries.

"How much farther?"

"Are we nearly there?"

"Can we have a rest?"

"I'm tired."

"I'm cold."

"I'm hungry."

"I feel sick."

"My feet hurt," piped the mousekins as they struggled along, and from the smallest, Love-in-a-Mist, came a final cry of "Mom! Stop! I can't go any farther."

Just at that moment Hyacinth saw a large squarish shape looming up in the corner of the big field.

"Come along, darlings!" she cried. "We're nearly there." And she ran forward to find herself at the foot of a great stack of straw bales. At that very minute an eerie wavering call sounded from the upper branches of a nearby hedgerow tree.

"Tu-whit!" it said. "Tu-whit!" and then "Ho-hoo-hoo-hoooooo!"

"Quickly!" cried Hyacinth. "Hurry, all of you!" And at the sound of her voice the tawny owl launched itself from its perch.

Frantically Robin at the rear urged on his exhausted children—Lily, Lilac, Lotus, Lupin, Lobelia, Laburnum, Larkspur, Lavender, and little Love-in-a-Mist—and frantically the mousekins scuttled toward safety.

"In here!" cried Hyacinth, diving into a gap between two straw bales, and in there they dashed as the owl swooped silently down, its talons spread, ready to grip, its great golden eyes fixed on the last in line, Ragged Robin.

From inside the safety of the stack Hyacinth heard him give a single piercing squeal, and then there was a horrid silence.

Hyacinth's heart was sore within her breast. He's been killed, she thought, my Robin's been killed, and it need never have happened. We should never have left

school. It's all my fault. I and I alone am to blame. And now I am a widow.

She gathered her mousekins about her. "Children," she said in tones of deepest woe, "your father has gone."

"Where's he gone, Mom?" said Lotus.

"West," said Hyacinth. "He has passed over."

"Over what, Mom?" said Lobella.

"Over the great divide," said Hyacinth. "He's had it."

"Mom," said Lupin. "What's he had?"

"Oh, for goodness' sake!" said Hyacinth sharply. "Daddy's dead."

There was a moment's silence and then, in a very small voice, "Poor Daddy," said little Love-in-a-Mist.

Suddenly Hyacinth thought she heard a distant cry. A muffled cry it was, coming from somewhere far back along the tunnels between the straw bales through which they had come.

"Hyce!" came the muffled cry. "Hyce! Where are you?"

"Robin's ghost," said Hyacinth to herself in an agony of spirit, "come to haunt me for the rest of my days."

But then the sound grew louder, and before long a familiar face appeared to them all. An untidy sort of face it was, with one battered ear, but it was solid flesh and blood nevertheless.

"Oh, Hyce!" said Ragged Robin. "That was a narrow squeak."

In fact the owl's dive had been a fraction of a second too late. When it landed in a flurry of loose straw at the foot of the stack, all that was still showing of Robin was his tail, that tail that had already been shortened in an old fight, and the best that the owl could do was to chop at it as the mouse disappeared.

"Robin!" cried Hyacinth, and "Daddy!" cried the nine mousekins.

"Oh, Robin!" said Hyacinth. "I thought I had lost you. I never was so hurt."

"Nor I," said Robin.

"I heard that awful squeal," said Hyacinth, "and I thought you had come to a sticky end."

"I suppose I have, in a way, Hyce," said Ragged Robin, and he turned himself around so that they could see.

All that was left of his tail was a blood-stained stump.

CHAPTER SEVEN

In Which Flora Sees a Ghost

"THERE IS NOT A MOUSE ALIVE anywhere in this school, not one," the headmistress had said at the staff meeting. She was wrong.

What's more, on the very next day there were two.

One, of course, was Flora, and the other belonged to Tommy, the naughtiest boy in the second-grade class.

Christmas is a time when people are sometimes given unsuitable presents. Often these are pets. Everyone knows that many puppies are bought by the wrong people for the wrong reasons and soon after discarded, often cruelly.

Lesser pets can suffer the same fate, and Tommy had been given a pet mouse as a Christmas present.

For a few days it was a novelty for him,

and he quite liked feeding it and watching it working away at the little treadmill that was fitted in its cage. But then he became bored with it. The pet mouse was bored too—that's why it spent its time in the treadmill—and no doubt in due course Tommy would have neglected it. But then he had a brilliant idea.

He remembered the disgust that the headmistress had shown upon finding mouse droppings on her register. And I bet she's scared stiff of mice, he thought (and the other teachers are, too, with a bit of luck). I'll take my mouse into school and let it go on her desk. I bet she'll have forty fits!

So it was that on the very first day after vacation that Tommy brought his mouse with him, secretly of course, for pets were not allowed in school. He brought it in a little cardboard box, which he hid in the locker where he kept his books. He did not tell any of his friends.

All morning he sat imagining the scene. He would wait till after lunch, till after the midday break. Then, when they came in from the playground, he would take the mouse out of its box and let it go on the headmistress's desk, just a moment before she entered the classroom.

Okay, so he'd be punished. He didn't care. It would all be worth it just to see her face and hear her scream!

But as everyone knows, the best-laid schemes of mice and men don't always quite work out. When Tommy came in from the playground at one o'clock and hurried to open the little cardboard box, it was empty. In one side of it a mouse-sized hole had been gnawed.

All that afternoon Tommy sat, waiting hopefully, his eyes darting about the second-grade classroom. The mouse must be around somewhere. Things might still work out all right if only he could spot it and catch it, at afternoon break perhaps. But there was no sign of it.

"Maybe it'll turn up tomorrow," Tommy said to himself. "And if it doesn't, what do I care? I'm tired of the stupid thing anyway."

Neither on the next day nor on those that followed was there any sign of Tommy's mouse, but Flora was getting into the swing of school. The bookshelf was proving to be a great success, both as a home and as a vantage point.

By peeping out at various spots between the loosely stacked books, Flora the first grader enjoyed a much wider range of vision than had Flora the kindergartner, stuck in the hole in the wall.

Now, as well as surveying the teacher's desk, she could also see what a number of children were doing at their worktables. There were more snatches of new books for her to read, and by watching carefully during math lessons, Flora came gradually to understand the symbols that stood for different numbers. Also, there was a large calendar on the opposite wall, with the dates in very big red figures, and by studying these Flora learned to count. But not, of course, beyond thirty-one.

While the children were in school, Flora was as happy as could be, busy with her lessons. And at playtime or during the lunch hour, when the classroom was empty, she would leave the bookshelf and scuttle about, climbing onto the tables and studying any book that had been left open.

In this way she learned a number of things not normally known to mice. For example, she read that the earth went round the sun, that David slew Goliath, that Paris was the capital of France, and that Henry VIII had six wives. She did not understand the full meaning of these interesting facts, but she stored them away in her memory in case they should come in handy one day.

Food, now that she was the only school mouse in the place, was much easier to come by. She soon learned the order in which the cleaning ladies did the hall and the various classrooms after school, and she usually contrived to nip round ahead of them, picking up the crumbs and bits of food that the children had dropped.

It was only when the school was empty of people and night fell that Flora was less than comfortable. Partly, she was lonely. She had always been independent by nature, but she found herself missing her parents and wondering about the nine new mousekins she had never as yet set eyes on. Where were they all now?

Partly, she was afraid as she thought about her own nine brothers and sisters, all dead and gone, and particularly of Sweet William who had died in the very classroom in which she now lived.

One stormy night of thunder and lightning, when the wind was howling around the old school, Flora sat remembering his horrible groans. What if the ghost of Sweet William should appear to me? she thought. She peered out between her books, and as she did so a flash of lightning lit up, just for a second, the first-grade classroom. But in that second Flora saw

clearly the figure that even now was cross-
ing the floor toward her.

It was the figure of a mouse, a mouse
whose eyes shone blood red in the glare of
light, a mouse whose coat was not the gray
brown of other, ordinary mice, but a pure
ghastly ghostly white!

Legend
~ OF ~
Sleepy
Hollow
~ BY ~
Washington Irving

CHAPTER EIGHT

In Which Buck Moves In

FLORA LET OUT A SQUEAL OF TERROR.

"Keep away from me, Sweet William, keep away!" she squeaked, and a grumpy voice answered, "Who are you calling Sweet William?"

Do ghosts talk? thought Flora.

"Are you a real mouse?" she asked.

"Of course I am," said the grumpy voice.

"But you're white."

"So what? Lots of pet mice are white."

"Oh," said Flora. "I didn't know."

"I daresay there are a lot of things you don't know," said the white mouse.

Flora was rather hurt at this. I bet I know more than he does, she thought, for her nose now told her she was addressing a male. She remembered something she had learned that very afternoon.

"I know the name of the mother of the

queen," she said. "Do you?"

"No," said the white mouse. "What is it?"

"The Queen Mother."

The white mouse made no reply to this piece of information. Another lightning flash showed Flora that he had turned his back on her and was sitting up and cleaning his whiskers.

He is rather rude, Flora thought.

After a while he said, "Well, what's your name?"

"Flora. What's yours?"

"Mother always called me Buck," said the white mouse.

Buck, thought Flora. That's silly. That's like a pig calling her son Boar, or a cow calling hers Bull.

"Why?" she said.

"Because I was the only boy among six of us. She gave my five sisters pretty names, but she just called me Buck, and Buck has stuck, worse luck."

He doesn't sound very happy, Flora thought. She ran down the wall beneath the bookshelf and approached the stranger.

"You don't sound very happy," she said.

"I'm not," said Buck, "nor would you be

in my place. A couple of weeks ago I was living comfortably in a pet shop, warm and clean and well fed. And then I was picked out—held up by my tail, I'll have you know—and given to a stupid boy. I could tell by the way he handled me that he knew nothing about animals, and then to cap it all he put me in a box and brought me to this place."

"And you escaped?" said Flora.

"Yes, and I've been trying to keep out of sight since. At least I'm free. The last thing I want is for that stupid boy to find me again. By the way, you're the first mouse I've met here."

"I'm the only mouse in the school," said Flora.

"So this is a school, is it?" said Buck.

"Yes," said Flora. "It's a place where they teach young human beings to read and write and do math and stuff like that."

"Reading? Writing? Math? It's all Greek to me," said Buck. "But it explains why there are so many of the noisy creatures about. It's a wonder that none of them has spotted me yet."

Especially as you're white, Flora thought.

The storm had moved away while they

were talking, the thunder distant now, and the wind's howl had dropped to a mere humming. Through the tall windows of the first-grade classroom came the first light of dawn, and Buck ceased his grooming and turned his pink eyes on Flora.

"That's better," he said. "Now I can see you properly. My night sight is very poor, I'm afraid—it's the same with all us pink-eyed whites, you know. We're none of us blessed with good vision."

Flora, whose sight was excellent by day or night, immediately felt sorry for him. And that was not all she felt. How handsome he is, she thought, so large and sleek. And those wonderful red eyes— they make me go quite weak at the knees. And that gleaming coat of his, white as the driven snow—how beautiful it is. And how dangerous! "It can only be a matter of time before he will be recaptured," she said to herself, "so conspicuous is he. And then I shall lose him. And I don't want to."

While she was thinking all these thoughts, Buck continued to stare at her without speaking. Then he asked, "Why do you live by yourself in the school?"

"I'm a school mouse," Flora said.

"Yes, but why are you alone?" said Buck. "I mean, I should have thought you'd have had lots of admirers, pretty girl like you."

"No," said Flora.

"Oh," said Buck.

There was quite a long silence as the two so different-looking mice crouched on the classroom floor, in broad daylight now.

At last Flora spoke. "Buck," she said.

"Yes?"

"I may call you Buck?"

"Of course, Flora."

"Are you planning to stay here, in the school?"

"Certainly I am," said Buck. "You, who have been free all your life, to go where you like and do what you please, can't imagine the joy of freedom to someone like me. My life so far has been one of imprisonment, but no longer."

"Then we must make plans," said Flora. "People will be coming in to the school before long, and they mustn't see you."

Then she had a thought. Recently she had come upon a natural history book open at a page about camouflage. She did not quite know how to pronounce the word, but she could see what it meant from the pictures. One was of a tiger, its striped coat blending into the jungle background, and one of a drab-colored bird, almost invisible on its nest among a tangle of tussocks.

"If you were to get your coat really dirty," she said, "you wouldn't be nearly as noticeable."

"No," said Buck. "No, Flora, I'm sorry but I draw the line at that. I have always prided myself on being well turned out. The slightest speck of dirt on my coat upsets me to no end. I can't bear a scruffy mouse."

You wouldn't think much of Father then, thought Flora, as she watched Buck fall once more to grooming himself.

"You'll have to be hidden then," she said, "for the whole of the school day. We must find somewhere safe, and quickly, too. Let me think."

He must go underground, she thought, under the floorboards somewhere, as Mother and Father did in the staff room. There, perhaps? No, it was too far away; she must have him close—surely there must be somewhere in this very classroom.

Flora began to run about, searching, and almost at once luck was with her. In one corner of the first-grade classroom stood a sink where the children washed up their brushes and pots after painting lessons. A hole had been cut in the floor to take the drainpipe that ran down from this sink, and around the edge of this hole there was ample room for a mouse to get down.

Flora got down and found that there was a comfortable space beneath, where Buck might be undisturbed save for the occasional gurgle of running water.

"Quick!" she called. "Down here, Buck."

"Now," she said when he had found her, "you'll just have to stay here all day and not make a sound. Have a good sleep; I would. I'll come and fetch you at the end of school."

"But, Flora," said Buck, "aren't you going to stay here with me?"

"No," said Flora. "You must remember, Buck, that I am a school mouse. I have an awful lot to learn."

"I don't quite understand," said Buck.

There was a distant noise as the front door of the school was unlocked.

"I can't explain now," said Flora hurriedly. "I've got to go, or I shall miss my lessons."

Buck's eyes glowed red in the darkness under the floorboards. "I shall miss you," he said softly.

CHAPTER NINE

In Which Robin Obeys Orders

MEANWHILE, BACK AT THE STACK, the school mouse family had settled in.

There was plenty of food, for in the straw were a great many grains of barley that the combine harvester had missed, and there were warmth and shelter among the bales. There was no shortage of comfort, but there was also no shortage of enemies.

Ragged Robin's wound had healed pretty well, but each night the cry of the tawny owl reminded him of his narrow escape. Other visitors to the stack included foxes and an old tomcat living wild.

"Just stay inside," said Hyacinth to the mousekins, "and you'll be safe from cat, fox, or owl. They cannot get in among the bales."

But someone else could.

One night, a week or so after the meeting of Flora and Buck, the straw stack was, as usual, a hive of activity. At the cold end of January it was home to a wide variety of rodents, and in the dozens of runways between the bales lived rats and voles, field mice, harvest mice, and shrews, together with a good many ordinary house mice and not forgetting the eleven school mice.

The tawny owl, looking down from its perch in an oak tree, saw a little animal at the base of the stack, scampering along the ground straight-bodied as though it had no legs. In color it was a reddish brown with a white underside, and it was no more than eight inches in length. For an instant it paused at an entrance hole between two bales, one forefoot lifted, its short tail erect. Then, even as the owl launched itself, the weasel disappeared into the stack.

The owl circled and flew up again onto its perch and stood with its back against the trunk of the oak, listening. So sharp was its hearing that it clearly heard the sudden panic-stricken scurrying and scuttling within, and then a single terrified squeak that died abruptly away.

Hyacinth heard it, too, from the nesting place she had chosen deep inside the stack.

Hastily she called the mousekins to her and took a roll call. All answered to their names but one. Laburnum was absent.

Just then Ragged Robin appeared, his eyes nearly popping out of his head.

"Oh, Hyce!" he cried. "It nearly got me!"

"What nearly got you?" said Hyacinth.

"Oh, it was horrible!" said Robin. "I saw it go by and it looked awful and it smelled awful and it was making a horrid hissing noise and I came across an old rat and I said, 'What is it?' and he said, 'Weasel,' and his teeth were chattering and his hair was standing on end and he was shaking with fright even though he must

have been five times the size of the thing and then it must have killed a mouse. I heard it squeak."

"Laburnum," said Hyacinth.

"But Mom," cried the eight remaining mousekins, "you said we'd be safe inside the stack; you said nothing could get in, that's what you said." Before Hyacinth could answer, they all heard the horrid hissing noise of which Robin had spoken, and in a blind panic the whole school mouse family fled in every direction.

For the bloodthirsty weasel it was a red-letter night. It snaked its way through the straw labyrinth, killing for the sake of killing, and Hyacinth's mousekins in particular were easy prey.

By the end of the night it had put paid to three more of them.

From then on, things went from bad to worse. Fear that the weasel might return led the survivors to risk a search for hiding places outside the straw stack, and as time went by, owl, cat, and fox accounted for four more. By the end of March the only survivors of the family of school mice were Hyacinth, Ragged Robin, and one remaining daughter, little Love-in-a-Mist, who had stuck close to her mother throughout.

"Nineteen children I have borne," said Hyacinth, "and only this poor mite to show for it."

"You're forgetting, Hyce," said Robin. "There's Flora."

"Oh yes. That stubborn girl."

"I wonder how she's getting on," said Robin.

Hyacinth looked thoughtfully at her mate. "I think we should find out," she said.

"Find out?" said Robin. "How can we find out? She is in the school. We are in the stack."

"Not for much longer, I hope," said Hyacinth. "It's a death trap."

Ragged Robin looked smugly at his wife. "It was you who brought us here, Hyce," he said.

Hyacinth looked angrily at her scruffy dog-eared tailless husband. "That's right, blame me for everything," she said.

"Mom," said Love-in-a-Mist, "why did we leave school?"

"It wasn't safe there," said Hyacinth. "There was poison."

"While out here," said Robin tartly,

"we've only got owls and cats and foxes and weasels."

"All right, all right," snapped Hyacinth. "We will go back. Providing Flora has survived. Go on, go and find out."

"Who, me?" said Robin.

"Well, you don't think I meant Love-in-a-Mist, do you?"

"It's quite a step," said Robin. "Right across the other side of that great field, a long way for an old chap like me but no distance for her young legs. And she's got a tail, what's more."

"Love-in-a-Mist," said Hyacinth. "Run away and play. I wish to speak seriously to your father."

So it was that some hours later a tailless mouse was to be seen making his nervous way over the field, across the playground, and into the school buildings. Ragged Robin was heading for the kindergarten classroom where he thought to find Flora, when suddenly a voice behind him said, "Hey, you!"

Robin turned to find himself facing a strange mouse, a mouse a good bit larger than himself, a mouse, what's more, with pink eyes and a coat of gleaming white, who was marching purposefully toward him.

"Hey, you!" said the white mouse again.

"Who, me?" said Robin.

"Yes, you, you shabby old bobtailed hasbeen. What do you want?"

"I want to see Flora."

"Not on your life!" cried the white mouse, and with a squeak of anger he threw himself upon the unfortunate Robin.

CHAPTER TEN

In Which Robin Comes Off Worse

IN HIS SALAD DAYS RAGGED ROBIN had been a scrappy fighter, but those times were long past. Youth and the advantage of weight were on Buck's side, as was the element of surprise in his assault, and Robin fared badly. He was especially handicapped by the lack of a tail, so important to a mouse's balance, and he gave ground in the face of his attacker's fury.

"Want to see Flora, do you?" growled Buck. "She's my Flora, understand? Mine!"

"But she's my Flora!" panted Robin, and then he let out a squeal of pain as the white mouse bit him through the foot.

The noise of the scuffle brought Flora rushing to the scene, a scene that filled her with horror. Outclassed by his young, strong opponent, Robin was indeed ragged. Battered and blood-flecked, he still

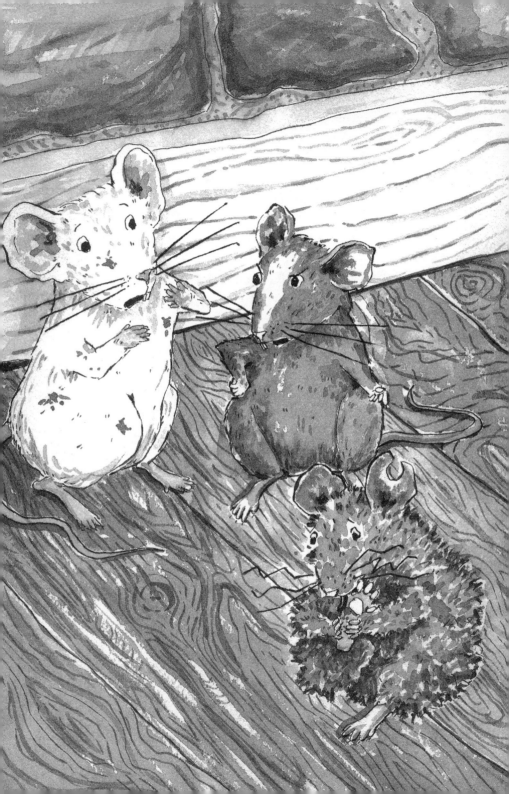

fought on desperately on three legs, but the outcome of the battle was obvious.

Flora thrust herself between the combatants. "Stop, Buck! Stop!" she cried. "Don't you know what you're doing?"

"Yes," said Buck. "I'm beating up this intruder, nasty scruffy old thing. What's more, he's gone and bled all over my clean coat. Said he wanted to see you, he did. What's he want with a young girl like you? He's just a dirty old mouse."

"He's not!" said Flora. "He's my father!"

"Your father?" said Buck, astonished.

"Yes, and you've hurt his poor foot. And you call yourself my boyfriend."

"Your boyfriend?" said Robin, amazed.

"And oh, oh," Flora went on, "you've bitten his tail off!"

"I didn't," said Buck, "did I?"

"No, Flora," said Robin. "He didn't do that. But it's a good job you turned up, or he'd have made an end of me."

"Oh, Father!" cried Flora. "Will you be all right? And where's Mother? And where are the mousekins? And why are you here?"

"I came to see you, Flora," said Robin. "Like I told what's his name here."

"Buck," said Flora. "He's called Buck.

And he's got something to say to you."

Buck looked up from cleaning the spots of blood off his coat. "I have?" he said.

"Yes," said Flora, and there was an echo of her mother in the tone of her voice and the set of her jaw. "You are going to say you are sorry."

"Shan't," said Buck.

"Very well," said Flora. "In that case I shall never squeak to you again." And she marched off.

"High-spirited girl," said Robin, licking his wounded foot. "Takes after her mother."

Buck looked curiously at this old wreck of a mouse. Flora's dad, he thought. Who'd have guessed, when she's so neat and pretty. "And angry," he said to himself. Maybe I'd better try to put things right, though I can't see there's any need to apologize. He should have said who he was in the first place. He cleared his throat.

"You put up a pretty good scrap," he said. "For an old guy, that is."

"I've won a few fights in my time," said Robin.

There was a silence while Buck cast about for something else to say.

"Foot hurt?" he asked at last.

"Yes," said Robin.

"Ah," said Buck.

Another silence ensued. It was light by now, but there was no need for concealment. It was spring vacation, and the school was empty.

"If you don't mind my asking," said Buck at last, "how did you lose your tail?"

"Owl," said Robin.

"Oh," said Buck.

He's not very talkative, he thought. What can I say to please the old devil? Oh yes, I know.

"Your daughter Flora," he said. "Prettiest girl I've ever seen."

Robin stopped his licking and looked up into the pink eyes. "Spitting image of her mother," he said.

"Really?"

"Yes. Hyacinth is a great beauty."

"Hyacinth? That's a nice name. By the way, I don't know yours."

"Robin."

"Robin," said Buck. "That's a nice name, too."

"You think so?"

"Definitely. And Flora, of course, is a lovely name."

"Keen on her, are you?"

"I certainly am, Robin," said Buck.

"And she's . . . um . . . fond of you?"

"Yes. I'm a lucky fellow."

You're a handsome fellow, thought Robin, with those pink eyes and that snow white coat. Not surprised she's fallen for you.

"I never could understand," he said, "why Hyacinth picked me. I wasn't the best-looking of mice then, and I'm certainly not now."

Poor old chap, thought Buck, with his busted ear and no tail and now I've gone and lamed him. Not surprised Flora blew her top.

"I'm sorry," he said.

"What's that?" said Robin.

"I'm sorry I knocked you about, Robin."

"Oh," said Robin. "Oh, that's all right. Decent of you to say so, er, Buck."

Flora had heard every word of this conversation. After she had flounced out, she hid and listened, and on hearing Buck's apology she came running back.

"Now, Father," she said, "tell me. How is everybody? And what are you doing here?"

So Robin related all that had happened since leaving school, while Flora listened with little cries of "Oh no!" and Buck's pink eyes bulged with horror at this tale of death and disaster.

"So I came back to see how things were here," finished Robin. "Or rather, your mother sent me. Which reminds me, I must report back to her at the straw stack. She'll be wondering what's happened to me, she and little Love-in-a-Mist. That is, if something awful hasn't already happened to them. I must go straightaway."

"You cannot, Father," said Flora. "You can't even put that foot to the ground, let alone travel all that way back."

"But someone must fetch them," said Robin.

"Let me," said Buck.

"Good of you to offer, my boy," said Robin, "but it would be suicide for a mouse of your color. No, no, I must go."

"You will do nothing of the sort," said Flora.

"But, Flora," said her father, "we cannot simply leave them there in that death trap."

"We will not," said Flora. "I shall go and fetch them."

CHAPTER ELEVEN

In Which Flora Takes a Journey

BEFORE THE OTHERS COULD open their mouths to protest, Flora was gone.

Her father, she knew, could not follow her, and Buck, she hoped, would not. What with his poor sight and his sense of smell much less sharp than that of a wild mouse, she shuddered to think what might befall him out in the open in broad daylight. "Or what might befall me for that matter," she said to herself. Nevertheless she pressed bravely on, hoping to sight the straw stack before too long.

In fact, she could hardly see beyond the end of her nose, so much had the spring grass grown. What she could do, though, was to hear something. At first it was just a distant rumble, but quickly it grew louder, until it became a roaring thundering deafening noise heading straight for her while the ground beneath her feet shook.

Flora cast a terrified glance behind her to see a huge red monster approaching. Leaping madly away to get out of its path, she came to a bank at the field's edge, a bank in which, she saw, there was a large hole.

Flora dived headlong into the hole as the monster went lumbering by. For a long while she crouched there, too frightened to move. Then at last she heard something approaching her from the inside of the burrow in whose mouth she sat, and before she could decide what to do, a large animal appeared. It was large—that is to say, to Flora's eyes—and brown in color, with a furry coat and big liquid eyes and long ears that stuck up.

"What's up then, mouse?" said the animal. It had two large front teeth, Flora could see, but something told her that it was not dangerous, and she held her ground.

"Sorry to intrude," she said, "but I was being chased by a red monster."

"Red monster!" said the animal. "What be you then—some kind of town mouse?"

"No," said Flora. "I'm a school mouse. And please, what are you?"

"You don't know?"

"No."

"Where you been all your life, mouse?"

"In school."

"You ain't learned much then. Never seen a rabbit before?"

R-a-b-b-i-t, thought Flora. Of course! I remember seeing a picture in that very first book I ever looked at.

"Only in a book," she said.

The rabbit shook his long ears in bewilderment.

"You soft in the head, mouse?" he said. "All this stuff about school mice and books and red monsters: anyone'd think you ain't never seen a tractor before neither."

T-r-a-c-t-o-r, thought Flora. Yes, that

was in the book, too.

"What was it doing?" she asked.

"Going down along to the stack," said the rabbit, "to get a trailer load of straw bales."

"My mother's living in the stack," Flora said.

"Haven't you got no daddy?" the rabbit said.

"He's in the school."

"They're separated, huh?"

"Well, yes, they are, just at the moment," said Flora. "That's why I'm out here—to fetch my mother and my little sister and take them back to school. They'll be safe there, I hope, and anyway I want them to meet my boyfriend. He's called Buck."

"Buck?" said the rabbit. "You got a rabbit for a boyfriend?"

"No, no, he's a mouse. He's ever so handsome. He's pure white, you know, snowy white, and he's got beautiful pink eyes."

"And six legs and a pair of dear little wings, I suppose," said the rabbit. "I got to hand it to you, mouse. You're the craziest. I dunno about school mice, seems to me

'tis more fool mouse," and with those parting words he turned and disappeared down
his burrow.

Meanwhile, down at the haystack, Hyacinth and Love-in-a-Mist were unwor-
ried at the sound of the tractor's approach.
They had grown used to its regular visits to
collect a load of straw. What they had not
bargained for was that one day, as the stack
diminished in size, they might become
part of the load.

That morning it so happened that they
had made their way to the very edge of the
stack, to watch out for Ragged Robin's return, when the tractor driver began to load
his trailer.

"Dratted mice!" he said, as he lifted a
bale and found two of the creatures hiding
beneath it, but before he could do anything, they had leaped onto the bed of the
trailer and hidden themselves among the
bales already there.

When the tractor returned across the field
with its load, Flora had been on the point
of leaving the shelter of the rabbit burrow.
But hearing it approach, she forced herself

to observe it carefully as it went by. "It is all part of my education," she told herself, "to learn about such things." She noted the features of the great red monster, its driver perched high in his cab, and she ran her eye down the load of straw bales.

Suddenly she saw, right at the bottom of the load, two anxious faces peeping out between a couple of bales on the bed. One, a small one, she did not recognize. The other she did.

"Mother!" yelled Flora at the top of her voice, and she ran out of the rabbit hole and scuttled along beside the tractor.

"It's our Flora," said Hyacinth to Love-in-a-Mist.

"Jump, Mother! Jump!" cried Flora.

"Jump, Lovey," said Hyacinth.

"But, Mom . . . ," said Love-in-a-Mist.

"No buts," said Hyacinth.

For a mouse, a leap from such a height is the equivalent of a man plunging off the top of a tall building. But mice fall light, and the lush grass cushioned their landing so that they bounced, unhurt.

"Flora!" said Hyacinth. "What are you doing out here?"

"Come to fetch you, Mother," said Flora.

"But why did your father not come back? I told him to."

"Is Dad all right?" said Love-in-a-Mist.

"You must be Love-in-a-Mist," said Flora. "You have got a long name, haven't you?"

"Mom usually calls me Lovey."

"Come on then, Lovey," said Flora. "We must all hurry back to school, and then I can explain everything."

"Are you still in kindergarten?" asked Hyacinth when they arrived at school.

"Oh no, Mother," said Flora. "I'm a first grader now." And she led the way to her classroom.

In her absence, Ragged Robin and Buck had spent their time in conversation.

Buck was feeling guilty at having wounded Flora's father, and Robin was touched at his obvious concern. "Don't worry, my boy," he said. "Least said, soonest mended." But in fact they said a great deal to one another.

Robin wanted to know all about pet mice and Buck about school mice. "It's this reading business that amazes me, Robin," he said. "I don't know how Flora does it. And she can count to thirty-one, whatever that means, and she knows a fantastic lot of things. Education, she calls it. I don't even know what the word means."

"Me neither, Buck," said Robin. "I've been a school mouse all my life, but you could count the things I know on the toes of one foot."

"Speaking of feet," Buck said, "you should be resting yours. Why not come on down to my place? You'll find it quite comfy."

So off they went to the first-grade classroom, and Robin followed Buck down the hole beneath the sink.

It was indeed a comfortable den, for Buck had pulled a good deal of the insulation off the water pipes, and the two mice took their ease on the most comfortable of thick beds of yellow felt. The time passed pleasantly as they chatted, and then at last they heard voices above.

"They're here!" said Robin, and he made his way up through the hole in the floorboards and limped, three-legged, toward his wife. "Hyce, my dear!" he cried. "You're back!"

Hyacinth regarded her scruffy husband

with a stern eye. "You've been fighting," she said.

"Well, yes," said Robin.

"How could you! You are too old for such behavior."

"Well, yes," said Robin.

"You started it, I've no doubt. You went and picked a fight with someone."

"Well, no," said Robin.

"And now you've got hurt. Why can't you act your age?"

"But Hyce . . . ," said Robin.

"I'd just like to get hold of the mouse that did it," said Hyacinth.

"But Mother . . . ," said Flora.

"No buts," said Hyacinth.

At this point Buck emerged from the hole. He looked, as usual, beautifully groomed, with not a hair out of place. His white coat gleamed, his whiskers were neatly combed.

He lowered the gaze of his pink eyes before Hyacinth's astonished stare. "I'm sorry," he said. "I am the mouse that did it."

For an instant Hyacinth stood stock still.

Then she leaped at Buck and fastened her needle-sharp teeth in the end of his nose.

CHAPTER TWELVE

In Which Hyacinth Makes an Apology

"YOUR BOMMY," SAID BUCK that night, "is a bost fierce bouse."

Flora licked his swollen snout tenderly. "I'm sorry," she said. "It all happened so quickly. I had no time to explain."

"She's bade a bess of by dose," said Buck.

"Lie down and rest," said Flora, arranging the felt bedding more comfortably around him. "I expect she'll say she's sorry in her own good time."

But Hyacinth was in no mood for apologies. That great white monstrosity of a mouse had bitten her poor little husband, so she had responded in kind. "A nose for a foot and a tooth for a tooth," she said to Robin, back in their old nest under the staff-room floor.

"You certainly clobbered him, Hyce,"

said Robin. His feelings were muddled. He felt sorry for his new friend, and at the same time pleased that his wife had sprung to avenge his injury. "You won't do it again though, will you?" he said. "Now that everything has been explained. I mean, he is one of the family now."

Hyacinth did not answer.

"I wish I had a boyfriend," said Lovey.

"You are much too young," said her mother. "Why, it seems only yesterday that you were born here, in this very spot."

"Buck's place is nice," said Robin. "It's much roomier than this and ever so well furnished. Why don't we move in with him and Flora—what d'you say, Hyce?"

But once again Hyacinth did not answer, and Robin knew better than to nag her.

As the next evening approached, only one of the five mice in the school had had a good day's sleep, and that was Lovey. Ragged Robin's foot and Buck's nose allowed them no more than a fitful doze, and Flora and Hyacinth were deep in thought. Each had a problem.

Under the boards in the staff room Hyacinth now wrestled with her conscience. Should she say she was sorry? She wasn't sorry, but should she say she was? How could they move in with Flora and Buck unless she did say so? What should she do?

Under the sink in the first-grade classroom Flora fretted about her future. "I shouldn't be here," she said to herself. "Spring vacation will soon be over, and it's time I became a second grader. I'm sure I could cope with the work. I want to move up, but I don't want to move house. What shall I do?"

As the light faded, Flora's thoughts were interrupted by the sudden appearance of Lovey. "There's a meeting, Flora," she said, "in the staff room. Now, Mom says." And away she went.

Flora and Buck made their way to the staff room, and as soon as they entered, Robin greeted them heartily. "Flora, dear!" he cried. "Buck my boy! How are you feeling?"

"Buch better, thag you, Robid," said Buck. "How about you?"

"Oh, I'm on the mend," said Robin. "Plenty of life in the old mouse yet."

An awkward silence followed. Neither of the male mice could think of anything further to say, and Flora's feelings toward her mother were less than kindly. She summoned us here, she thought, so let her get on with it.

After a while Hyacinth spoke. "Flora," she said heavily. "I owe you an apology."

"Me, Mother?" said Flora, looking sideways at Buck's nose.

"Yes," said Hyacinth. "I was hasty. I did not realize that this . . . person . . ."

"Buck," said Flora. "His name is Buck."

". . . that Buck was a friend of yours."

"It's not me you should be apologizing to, Mother," said Flora.

"But . . . ," began Hyacinth.

"No buts," said Flora in so Hyacinth-like a way that Robin was filled with delight. If a mouse could wag its tail like a dog, he'd have wagged his, if he'd had one.

"After all," said Flora, "if we are all to live together as one happy family, we don't want any more bad blood."

"Or any more good blood," said Robin.

"Well, that was really why I called this meeting," said Hyacinth hastily, "to see if you would be willing—you and Buck, that is—for your father and Lovey and me to share your accommodation. It's very comfortable and roomy, I hear, and it would be nice to be all together, wouldn't it?"

"On one condition, Mother," said Flora firmly.

"What's that?"

"Say you're sorry to Buck."

"It doesn't batter," said Buck. "Least said, soonest bended, eh, Robid?"

Robin did not answer. Go on, Hyce, he thought, say it, even if you don't mean it. It'll do me a power of good to hear you eating humble pie.

Hyacinth looked at the white mouse's still swollen snout. She took a deep breath.

"Buck," she said. "I am sorry that I bit your nose." And to her surprise, she found she meant it.

"Don't bention it," said Buck.

"Good old Hyce," said Robin.

"Let's all go to our place," said Flora.

"Yippee!" cried Lovey, and away they went.

*   *   *

The last few days of spring vacation slipped by pleasantly enough. Both Robin's and Buck's injuries healed well, and the white mouse found himself thoroughly accepted by Flora's family.

He and Robin were already firm friends, and for the little Lovey he was the perfect big brother. The way to Hyacinth's heart, he found, was flattery.

Accustomed as she was to nothing better than such compliments as "good old Hyce," she was delighted when, for instance, Buck passed a remark on the beauty of her eyes. "Oh, the depth of blackness in those shining orbs, Hyacinth," he murmured, fixing her with his pink ones, and she bridled with pleasure.

Only Flora was restless. As the end of spring vacation drew near, she haunted the second-grade classroom. She was determined to move up a grade, yet she did not want to leave the comfortable home under the first-grade sink.

Then, on the very last day of vacation, she found the solution. The second-grade classroom was by far the biggest in the school, and one end of it had been set aside as a library area. Here were not only well-stocked bookshelves, but also a large table on which various books of interest were always left open to encourage children to look through them. There were atlases and dictionaries and encyclopedias and many others.

Flora was standing in front of one of these, polishing up her reading skills, ready for school to begin again. It was an illustrated dictionary, open at pages dealing with the letter *C*. The picture was of a man in a suit, carrying a rolled umbrella and a briefcase and in the act of stepping into a railway carriage. It meant nothing to Flora, but she read the words beneath.

C o m m u t e r
One who travels daily from home to place of work, returning home at the end of the day.

Place of work, thought Flora. Well, for me that now means the classroom. So I won't have to leave home. I can commute to work and back each day.

Commuter: one who travels daily from home to place of work, returning home at the end of the day.

Compass: an instrument for showing direction with magnetic points.

CHAPTER THIRTEEN

In Which Flora Has a Brainstorm

SCHOOLCHILDREN LOOK FORWARD to vacation and grumble about having to go back to school.

School mice look forward to school and are less happy when it's closed and they have the place to themselves. To be sure, it's nice to be able to run about wherever they like, and the peace and quiet is pleasant, but food at holiday time is much harder to come by.

Like all mice, Flora and her family could eat most things, but when there were no children around, their diet wasn't nearly as varied. They needed to venture outside to gnaw at roots and bulbs, and they ate a great many insects, wood lice in particular being especially crunchy, but vacations were still a thin time.

For the school mice, then, that first day

after spring vacation ended was quite a treat. Flora's knowledge of the cleaning ladies' routine meant that she could direct the family to rooms as yet unswept: here they quickly snapped up cookie crumbs and apple cores and spilled fragments of potato chips of various flavors (cheese-and-onion being the favorite) before the arrival of vacuum and broom and dustpan-and-brush.

That first day in the new classroom led Flora to another breakthrough. Here there was no handy hole in the wall as in kinder-garten, no convenient bookshelf as in first grade, and already it was plain to her that the library area would be her happiest hunting ground in her search for knowl-edge.

At lunchtime and at both the morning and afternoon breaks, she came out of hid-ing and ran busily about the library table, studying the open books.

One of these, the same illustrated dictio-nary in which she had found "commuter," had been used that very day and was no longer open at the letter *C*. The user by chance had been Buck's former owner.

Tommy, as usual, was making a nuisance

of himself, and the headmistress had sent him to the library table and told him to sit quietly and look at a book.

Tommy had flicked the pages about aimlessly until he chanced upon a picture that interested him. It was of a cowboy astride a madly bucking bronco. He went into a daydream in which he defeated all comers at the rodeo, and he left the book open there.

The word that happened to catch Flora's eye was the one immediately before "rodeo."

R o d e n t

it said. Flora read on.

Rodents have distinctive chisellike
teeth. These teeth grow throughout
life as they are worn away by gnawing.
Common rodents are rats and mice,
and the first warning sign that a building is infested by them is the discovery
of their droppings. Poison may then
be used against these pests.

Musmors, thought Flora! Don't I know it! And she remembered poor Sweet William and all the others who had eaten the dreaded blue pellets.

"That's why the people used the poison," she said to herself, "because they found mouse droppings about the school. They mustn't find ours."

When the commuter arrived home from work, she told the others what she had read.

"Then we must be careful not to leave our droppings about in the future," said Hyacinth.

"That's all very well, Hyce," said Robin, "but a mouse has got to do what a mouse has got to do."

"Perhaps we should use just one place— under the floorboards?" said Buck.

"It'd get ever so stinky," said Lovey.

"I'll think of something," said Flora.

While the others were out foraging (under strict orders not to leave any evidence about), Flora lay in the hole beneath the sink, pondering the problem. She happened to be facing toward the drainpipe, and in her mind's eye she saw the wastewater pouring down inside, carrying away the rinsings of paint pots and brushes and the dirt from childish hands. Where to? she thought. Where does the gurgling water go?

Bestirring herself, she set out to follow

the line of the pipe under the floor. She knew that it took a right-angled turn and went along what was, so to speak, the side wall of their quarters, but she had never explored its course farther. Through a sizable hole in the outer wall of the school it disappeared at last, emerging, Flora found, above a drain in which was set a metal grating.

"Perfect!" said Flora. "The most modern form of sanitation, a toilet, where all will be flushed away. Here shall all our droppings drop."

And from that day on, they did, each mouse making the short journey to the drain hole whenever he or she felt the call of nature.

"A great idea that, don't you think?" said Buck a week or so later, when Flora, having first paid a visit to the drain, had commuted to work.

"She's no fool, our Flora," said Hyacinth.

"It's all this education," said Ragged Robin. "I never had none."

"You never had *any*, Dad," corrected Lovey.

Robin flared up at this piece of cheek from his younger daughter.

"You keep your trap shut, miss," he said.

"Robin!" said Hyacinth warningly, for this was bad language among mice, and Lovey moved behind her mother for luck.

But later that evening, when Flora had returned from her classroom and the others were going out and about, Lovey stayed behind for a moment.

"Flora," she said.

"Yes, Lovey?"

"You're educated, aren't you?"

"Well, not properly. Not yet. I'm getting

to know all sorts of things, but there's an awful lot left to learn."

"Like what?" said Lovey.

"Well," said Flora, "like geography and history and science and maybe even French. They had a French lesson today, the second grade did. It was ever so interesting. D'you know what the French for 'mouse' is?"

"No," said Lovey. "I don't know anything much. You're lucky, you are." And she ran off to find the others.

She's right, thought Flora, I *am* lucky. I don't suppose there's another mouse on the face of the earth that knows as much as I do already. But I can't talk much about my lessons to the others because they wouldn't understand.

Imagine asking Father to count to thirty-one!

Or asking Mother what's the capital of England.

And my Buck may be handsome, but he doesn't know much more than Lovey does, really. They're all uneducated. And why? Because there's no one to teach them.

Thankfully the school was, of course, empty of people at that moment, because suddenly Flora let out a loud, excited squeak.

"Yes, there is!" she cried. "There's me! I'll start evening classes for them all! I won't be just a school mouse. I'll be the world's first ever schoolteacher mouse."

CHAPTER FOURTEEN

In Which Lovey Plays Truant

FLORA'S FIRST EVENING CLASSES WERE not a great success.

Lovey was keen to learn, certainly. She was curious about things, like Flora, though not as bright.

Buck wanted to be taught, the better to understand some of the subjects that Flora knew so much about. He wished her to be proud of him.

But with Hyacinth and Robin it was a different matter. They say you shouldn't teach your grandmother to suck eggs, and at first it seemed to Flora that you shouldn't try to teach your parents anything.

Hyacinth felt she was being patronized. "You, teach me?" she said to Flora when she was told of the scheme. "I could teach you a thing or two, my girl," but she came along all the same, not wanting to be left

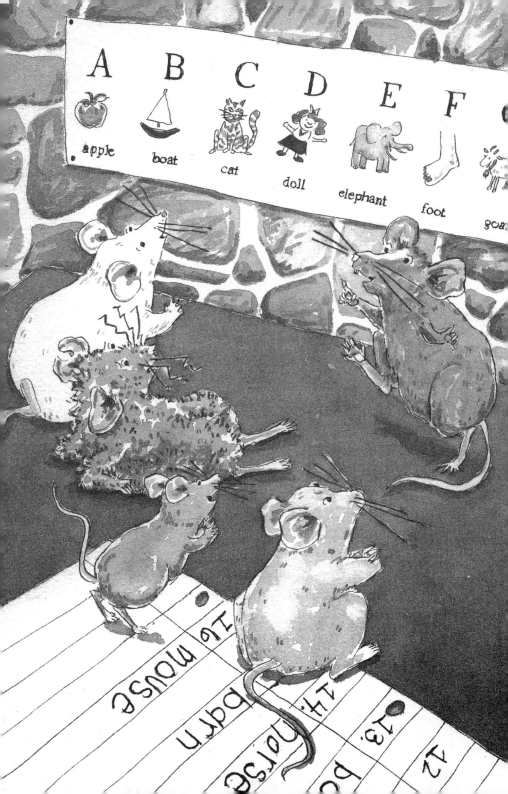

behind in the quest for knowledge.

As for Ragged Robin, he was willing but dim. He feared very much that he would be the dunce and that the others would look down on him.

The lessons took place in the kindergarten classroom.

Since Flora's days in kindergarten, the teacher had put up on the wall a large picture alphabet, the writing on it so big as to be clearly visible even to Buck's poor eyesight.

"I have brought you here," said Flora, confronting her class of three school mice and one pet mouse, "because the first and most important thing, for mice or humans, is to learn to read. Once you can do that, there is no limit to what you can get into your heads."

Robin shook his doubtfully.

"And before you can learn to read," Flora went on, "you must learn your alphabet. There it is. Now, then, the first letter of the alphabet is *A*."

"A what?" asked Hyacinth.

"Just listen, please, Mother," said Flora, "and don't interrupt. The second letter is *B*."

"A bee!" said Robin in a pleased voice. "I've seen them! Nearly got stung once."

"No, no," said Flora. "Just wait, Father, you don't understand."

"I knew I wouldn't," said Robin dolefully.

"And the third letter of the alphabet is C."

"See," said Buck. "Yes, I see."

"I don't," said Lovey. "I'm muddled. Start again, Flora."

That first lesson was hard going for everyone, but then Flora devised a way of teaching them the alphabet that was more fun. She invented a rhyme and made them learn it by heart. It went like this:

A B C D E F G
Oh, what clever mice are we!
H I J K L M N
Mice are just as bright as men.
O P Q R S T U
And to prove that this is true,
V and W X Y Z
that's the alphabet, you see!

Thanks to this method, Flora's class more or less mastered their ABCs, though Robin was sometimes apt to get his tongue in a twist. Now they could actually begin to learn to read.

For Flora, the rest of that spring was a hard slog. By day she educated herself, and in the evenings she taught her class. But she had not the advantages of the human teacher. She could not select the proper books from the shelves. Turning the pages of those she found lying about was not at all easy, and of course she could not make use of the blackboard.

But gradually, as time passed, her pupils began to recognize some common word or other, Lovey in particular making quite good progress.

"She can almost read," said Flora to herself, "but I'm not so sure about the others. There's a lot of guessing going on. I ought to test them. On a very simple book, of course."

And that, by chance, was what she found.

Though the school itself was very old, most of the books in the kindergarten classroom were quite modern. But one or two remained that must have been there from the beginning.

Flora found just such a one when nosing

around the shelves. She cocked her head sideways to read the title on the spine:

My Very First Reading Book

it said.

Excellent, thought Flora, it shall be theirs.

By pushing and pulling at it, the five of them managed to dislodge it from the shelf, and it fell on the floor, open.

"Ah!" cried Flora. "What luck! There are several short simple sentences on these pages. Now I want you all to study them carefully—there are no pictures here to help you—and then I shall ask each of you in turn to read a sentence out loud to the rest of the class. It will be your very first test, to see how well you can read. Mother, will you read the top line, please?"

Hyacinth studied the first line.

The boy played with his kite.

She recognized the word "boy," which she had often come across.

"It's about a boy," she said.

"Yes, good," said Flora. "What is the boy doing?"

"Give me a hint," said Hyacinth.

"Something up in the sky," said Flora.

"The boy is flying," said Hyacinth hopefully.

"Yes, well, good try, Mother," said Flora, and she read the sentence correctly.

"Flying his kite," said Hyacinth. "Yes, that's what I was going to say."

"Now, Father," said Flora. "Try the next line."

Robin looked nervously at the second sentence.

Meg has a nice new doll.

He recognized the word "a," but the rest was a mystery. I bet it's one of those ones we learned, he thought.

"Mice are just as bright as men," he said.

"Not quite," said Flora. "Buck, can you read it?"

"Not really," said Buck. "The print is so small. My eyesight, you know."

So Flora read that one out and then asked Lovey to try the third sentence, which was

The cat sat on the mat.

And slowly but quite correctly, Lovey read it!

"Wonderful!" cried Flora. "Good girl, Lovey!"

"That can't be right," said Robin grumpily. "I'm sure it should be 'The cat sat on the rat.' Anyone can see that makes much more sense."

Flora kept on with *My Very First Reading Book* for the remainder of the year. Each evening the mice pulled it down and each morning the kindergarten teacher, much surprised, put it back on the shelf. She tried to find out which child was responsible, but "Not me, miss!" was all she got.

She would have been even more surprised could she have seen what went on one warm June evening toward the end of the school year.

Flora had been taking a nap in the family home after her day's studies. She told the others she would meet them in the kindergarten classroom later.

She woke and stretched, thinking that perhaps she would try a little number work with the class. Here there was a calendar, too, and Lovey at least, she felt sure, would soon get the hang of counting.

When she arrived, it was to find that *My Very First Reading Book* had already been pulled down, and she was just in time to hear Buck say, very slowly, with long pauses between words,

"Spot is good. Good dog, Spot."

"Buck!" she cried. "That was brilliant! You'll be catching up with Lovey at this rate."

Hyacinth looked around. "Where is Lovey?" she said.

"Don't know," said Robin.

"I saw her not long ago," said Buck.

"Lovey!" they all squeaked.

But there was no answer, so they searched the school, calling and calling and looking everywhere.

But Lovey was gone.

CHAPTER FIFTEEN

In Which All Ends Happily

THE SCHOOL YEAR ENDED. The children and the teachers went home. The cleaning ladies cleaned up. The caretaker locked up. Once more the school mice had the school to themselves. But now there were only four of them.

Buck felt sad. Because she was small for her age and, of course, because she was Flora's sister, he had grown fond of Lovey and her cheeky ways.

Ragged Robin was ill tempered. "Life's not fair," he said to Flora. "Why do all these misfortunes happen to us?"

"Come and read to me, Father," said Flora. "It'll take your mind off things."

"Read?" said Robin. "Certainly not. I am on vacation."

Hyacinth seemed less worried than the others. Still, she went about in a preoccupied manner and was choosy about her food, developing a sudden addiction to soap, which she nibbled at in the sink.

Flora thought hard about Lovey's chances of survival. "They're not good," she said to herself. "Why she went I've no idea, but she'll live to regret it. Or rather, she won't live."

A French phrase book chanced to be lying open on the library table, and as Flora was studying it, she saw something that seemed to sum up the situation.

Adieu—farewell, good wishes at a
final parting.
Au revoir—good-bye until we meet
again.

But I'm afraid we shan't meet again, thought Flora. Adieu, Lovey. Later that day she was alone with Buck.

"Well," she said, "it looks like the end of my evening classes for the moment. Lovey's gone, Father flatly refuses to come, and Mother says she's too busy, though I can't see it myself. That only leaves you."

"A class of one," said Buck.

"Yes."

"That means you could devote yourself

116

to me. If you were willing."

Oh, Buck, thought Flora, I am devoted to you, you great white handsome beast!

"Of course I'm willing," she said. "I'd do anything for you; you know that."

Buck's pink eyes seemed to turn even redder. "Oh, Flora!" he breathed, and their whiskers mixed as they touched noses.

The weather was very hot, even at night, and since there was no need for caution, the school mice took their ease wherever they fancied, always remembering, of course, to return to the drain outside whenever nature called.

Only Hyacinth remained in the hole under the sink in the first-grade classroom, in so tetchy a mood that Robin took himself off to the old staff-room den for a bit of peace and quiet.

As for Flora and Buck, they decided to make use of the hole in the wall over the teacher's desk in the kindergarten classroom. It was cool and airy, and handy for the schoolteacher mouse and her solitary pupil.

About halfway through the summer, they were sitting together on the desk, bathed in a glow of contentment. Both teacher and pupil had good reason to be happy, for Buck, with his back turned to the calendar on the wall, had just succeeded in counting to thirty-one.

"I must tell Mother!" Flora said. "Don't move. Have a rest. You've earned it."

"Mother!" she called down the hole under the sink. "What do you think? Buck can count to thirty-one."

"Six is all I can manage," replied Hyacinth. "Come and have a look."

"Oh, Mother!" cried Flora when she saw the half dozen newborn babies, fat and pink and naked and hideous. "They're beautiful!"

"Fetch your father," said Hyacinth. "He's in the staff room."

Ragged Robin was not pleased at being summoned. "Now what have I done wrong?" he said to Flora.

"Nothing wrong, Father," said Flora.

"It's a nice surprise."

And to Robin, it was. "Hyce!" he cried when he saw this third crop of sons and daughters. "You never told me! I never knew!"

"Well, now you do," said Hyacinth shortly.

A horrid thought occurred to Robin, whose knowledge of heredity was sketchy. "Have they all got tails?" he asked.

"Poor Father," said Flora to Buck later in the hole in the wall. "He always says the wrong things, and then Mother gets furious with him."

"I'm glad you don't get furious with me," said Buck.

"You always say the right things," said Flora.

"Flora!" said Buck fondly, and immediately the word seemed to echo through the school. "Flora! Flora! Flora!" But the echo was more high-pitched, and the tone of it was familiar.

"It's Lovey!" cried Flora, and she ran down to the floor, Buck following. "In here, Lovey!" she called. "We're in the kindergarten classroom!"

In a moment the small figure of Lovey

appeared in the doorway. "I'm back!" she said. "Wait there. I'll fetch my friend."

"I didn't know you had a friend," said Flora.

"I didn't," said Lovey, "but I have one now. I'll just go and get him. He's a bit shy."

Flora and Buck looked at one another, but before they could speak, Lovey returned. Following her, rather reluctantly, was an even smaller mouse.

"This is Haycorn," said Lovey. "Haycorn, this is my sister Flora and her boyfriend Buck."

Haycorn took one look at Buck and turned tail, ready to flee, but Lovey reassured him. "It's all right," she said. "Buck's ever so nice. He's just white, that's all; he can't help it."

"Lovey," said Flora. "We've all been worried stiff. Wherever have you been all this time?"

"I've been down at the farm," said Lovey. "There's Mom and Dad, and there's you and Buck, and I said to myself, 'Come along, Love-in-a-Mist, my girl. It's time you started living up to your name.' So I went down to the farm on a nice misty evening, and who should I meet but Haycorn. He's a

farm mouse, you see, but I've been telling him he'll like it up here."

"I'm sure he will," said Flora and Buck with one voice.

"You will, won't you, Haycorn?" said Lovey.

"Yes, Lovey," said the very small mouse in a very small voice.

"And you'll come to Flora's class with us and learn to read."

"Yes, Lovey," said Haycorn.

"He may not want to," said Flora.

"He will," said Lovey. "Come along now, Haycorn. I'll introduce you to Mom and Dad."

"Oh, by the way," said Flora. "Mother's had six more babies."

"Oh, goody!" cried Lovey. "I adore babies. I just can't wait."

"Wait for what, Lovey?" said Haycorn.

Lovey gave a squeak of amusement. "He's very young," she said to Flora, "but he'll learn." And off she dashed, followed by her little swain.

"Fancy!" said Flora. "You have to admire her, Buck. Off she goes without telling a soul, finds her way to the farm, and picks up a boyfriend."

"She practically could pick him up," said Buck, "he's so small. Not much more than a baby really. And speaking of babies, I haven't seen those new ones yet."

"D'you want to?" said Flora.

"Oh yes. Lovey's not the only one who's fond of babies. I just wish . . ." And then he stopped.

"Just wish what, Buck?" said Flora.

"Oh, nothing," said Buck. He sighed.

"You've got your career," he said.

"Yes, indeed," said Flora. "What with you and Mother and Father and Lovey and Haycorn and before long Mother's new six, I shall have a big class to teach, a class of . . . well, you do the sum, Buck. How many?"

"Eleven," said Buck.

"Well done," said Flora. "You may have started life as a pet mouse, but you're learning fast. I'm proud of you. Your reading especially is coming on a treat. Which reminds me, I remember finding something in *My Very First Reading Book* that I want to show to you now. Help me get it off the shelf."

When the book had fallen to the ground, Flora began to turn the pages with her nose, looking at each until she found the one she wanted. "Ah yes, here it is," she said at last. "Read me this sentence, will you, Buck—the one I've got my paw on?"

"Children are a great blessing,"

read Buck, with a little help from his teacher.

"Would you agree?" asked Flora.

Buck stared at her across the pages of *My Very First Reading Book*. "You mean . . . ?" he said softly.

"I mean," said Flora, "that we are to be blessed. Shortly before the start of the next school year, I reckon."

"Oh, Flora!" said Buck. "How marvelous! And what extraordinary children they will be, with your brains (and your beauty, thought Flora) and with you to teach them. Why, there will be no limit to their scholarship. Oh, Flora, you have made me the happiest white mouse in the world."

"And you," said Flora, "have made me the happiest school mouse."